JACKIE CHAN

ADVENTURES ™ #4

Enter ... the Viper

Other Jackie Chan Adventures

THE DARK HAND
JADE'S SECRET POWER
SIGN OF THE OX

JACKIE CHAN ADVENTURES™ #4

Enter...the Viper

A novelization by Jacqueline Carrol
based on the teleplay 'Enter...the Viper'
written by David Slack

PUFFIN BOOKS

PUFFIN BOOKS

Published by the Penguin Group
Penguin Books Ltd, 80 Strand, London WC2R 0RL, England
Penguin Putnam Inc., 375 Hudson Street, New York, New York 10014, USA
Penguin Books Australia Ltd, 250 Camberwell Road, Camberwell, Victoria 3124,
Australia
Penguin Books Canada Ltd, 10 Alcorn Avenue, Toronto, Ontario, Canada M4V 3B2
Penguin Books India (P) Ltd, 11 Community Centre, Panchsheel Park,
New Delhi – 110 017, India
Penguin Books (NZ) Ltd, Cnr Rosedale and Airborne Roads, Albany,
Auckland, New Zealand
Penguin Books (South Africa) (Pty) Ltd, 24 Sturdee Avenue, Rosebank 2196,
South Africa

Penguin Books Ltd, Registered Offices: 80 Strand, London WC2R 0RL, England

www.penguin.com

First published 2002

2

TM and © 2002 Adelaide Productions, Inc.
All rights reserved

Set in 19 on 23pt Columbus MT

Made and printed in England by Clays Ltd, St Ives plc

Except in the United States of America, this book is sold subject to the condition that it
shall not, by way of trade or otherwise, be lent, re-sold, hired out, or otherwise circulated
without the publisher's prior consent in any form of binding or cover other than that in
which it is published and without a similar condition including this condition being
imposed on the subsequent purchaser

British Library Cataloguing in Publication Data
A CIP catalogue record for this book is available from the British Library

ISBN 0–141–31500–8

The Adventure Continues . . .

Hi! I'm Jackie. I'm an archaeologist. I study ancient treasures to learn about the past.

A legend says that twelve stone charms are scattered across the globe. Magical talismans!

Each holds a different kind of magic. All twelve together have incredible power!

My big adventure began when I discovered the rooster talisman. It was in the centre of a golden shield I found in Bavaria, Germany.

I didn't know that an evil group called The Dark Hand was looking for it. Or that they wanted to use the magic of the twelve talismans to rule the Earth.

But now I do. And it's up to me to protect the world from their evil plan. I must find all the talismans and keep them safe.

I already have the rooster talisman. And I found the ox too. The snake talisman is in a New York City museum and I heard The Dark Hand is going to steal it!

I have to get there first!

Chapter 1

'You must let me have the snake talisman!' Jackie Chan pleaded.

He waved his hands as he spoke to the director of a famous New York City museum. 'The talisman is very valuable! It is not safe here!'

Jackie pointed to a nearby display. A small, eight-sided stone with a snake carved into it sat on top of a marble pedestal.

The small stone was one of twelve

ancient Chinese charms that had been scattered across the globe. All of the talismans were magical. They brought amazing power to whoever possessed them.

A group of evil men called The Dark Hand wanted the talismans. Their leader, Valmont, was on a mission to capture them all. If The Dark Hand possessed all twelve, they would be able to control the world!

'You must let me have it,' Jackie repeated. 'It is only a matter of time before The Dark Hand tries to take it!'

The director's lips curled into a sneer. 'Thank you, Mr Chan, but we know how to keep things safe. We are also guarding the world famous Pink Puma Diamond.'

The director pointed to another pedestal. On top of it, inside a glass case, sat an enormous pink gem.

'Whoa!' Jackie exclaimed. 'It's huge! It must be worth a fortune!'

'It is.' The director sniffed. 'If we can guard this diamond, we can guard the talisman too!'

Jackie shook his head. This guy had no clue how clever – or how dangerous – The Dark Hand could be.

'But you don't understand,' Jackie said. 'The talisman is powerful! It –'

'Good day, Mr Chan,' the director interrupted. He turned and walked away.

'Great,' Jackie muttered. He made his way to the museum exit. 'Why doesn't anyone ever believe me when

I – oof!' He bumped into a large man.

The man stumbled. Something fell from his jacket and shattered on the floor.

'So sorry!' Jackie bent down and picked up the pieces of a tiny camera. 'Oh, no! I broke your camera,' he declared. 'I –' Then he gasped. 'Wait a minute. This is a *spy* camera!'

'*Chan!*' the man snarled.

Jackie looked up. It was Ratso, one of the members of The Dark Hand! 'Hey!' Jackie shouted.

Ratso turned and ran.

Jackie chased after him – right out the doors of the museum.

Meanwhile, a woman with long dark

hair and a large hat stared at the Pink Puma Diamond. It glittered under its glass display case.

The woman pressed a finger to the star-shaped pin on the front of her coat.

Click. Click. Click. A tiny camera hidden inside the pin took shots of the famous gem.

The woman smiled as she gazed at the diamond.

Soon, she thought. *Soon the Pink Puma will belong to me.*

Chapter 2

Jackie burst out of the museum. He saw Ratso racing along the crowded pavement. Ratso bumped and crashed into people as he tore down the street.

Jackie followed him, dodging and weaving through the crowd. He was closing in.

Then Ratso turned into an alley.

Jackie chased after him and saw him climbing over a tall chain-link fence.

With a burst of speed, Jackie leaped and sprang to the top of the fence. He did a somersault in mid-air, then dropped to the other side of the fence – right in Ratso's path!

Ratso growled and threw a punch at Jackie.

Jackie dodged to the side. Then, lightning-fast, he grabbed hold of the bottom of Ratso's coat and pulled it up over Ratso's head.

'Yaiiii!' Ratso yelled as Jackie whirled him around and around.

Riiip! The bottom of the coat tore off in Jackie's hands. Ratso was free! He took off down the alley.

Riiing! A loud noise came from the coat in Jackie's hands. 'Aahh!' Jackie yelped in surprise.

The coat rang again. *Oh!* Jackie thought. *It must be a mobile phone.* Someone was calling Ratso!

Jackie found the phone and flipped it open. 'Uh...yeah?' he muttered. He tried his best to imitate Ratso's voice.

'Is your mission complete, Ratso?' a smooth voice asked.

Jackie almost dropped the phone. That voice belonged to Valmont, the evil leader of The Dark Hand!

Chapter 3

'I said, did you finish your mission?' Valmont repeated.

'Uh ... yeah,' Jackie replied in a rough voice.

'Excellent!' Valmont said. 'Then we'll take the talisman from the museum tonight at midnight.'

'*Tonight?*' Jackie cried.

'Is there a problem, Ratso?' Valmont asked. He sounded angry.

'Uh . . . no, boss,' Jackie replied.

'No problem at all.' Jackie clicked off the phone.

But I do have a problem, he thought. *I need a plan to save the snake talisman – fast!*

Later that day, Jackie sat on his bed in his hotel room. He picked up the phone and called his friend, Captain Augustus Black. Black was the head of Section Thirteen, a top secret group that fought crime. Especially crimes done by The Dark Hand.

'They're moving in at midnight,' Jackie reported.

'OK,' Captain Black replied. 'I'll get my people on it right away. Keep an eye on the museum until they arrive. If The Dark Hand *does* steal the talisman, *stay on their tails*. I'll be in touch.'

Wait around? Let The Dark Hand steal the talisman? No way! Jackie unzipped his suitcase. He pulled out a black sweatshirt.

A girl's voice called from the other side of the room. 'Whatcha gonna do, Jackie?'

Jackie turned to see Jade, his eleven-year-old niece. She had the extension phone in her hand.

Jackie sighed. No matter how hard he tried, he couldn't keep Jade from getting into trouble. Now she was listening in on his conversations! Where did she get such bad manners?

'Are you going to sneak into the museum and steal the snake talisman before the bad guys do?' Jade asked.

'*Steal?* No way!' Jackie told her. 'I don't *steal*! That's crazy, Jade.'

Jackie put on his black sweatshirt and a black ski cap. Then he stuffed a sheet, a screwdriver and a small Statue of Liberty souvenir into his black gym bag.

'You *are*!' Jade cheered. 'You totally *are* going to steal it! Can I come with you, Jackie? Please?'

'No,' Jackie told her. Jade had managed to get involved in every one of Jackie's fights with The Dark Hand. But not this time, he promised himself.

'Jaaackie!' Jade got on her knees. 'Pleeease?' she begged. 'Tomorrow's Thanksgiving! Where's your Turkey Day spirit?'

Jackie squatted down in front of her. 'Jade, I really want to spend time with you, but you can't come with me tonight.' He patted her on the head. 'I promise I'll take you to the Thanksgiving Day Parade tomorrow.'

Jade sighed. She flopped down on her bed and folded her arms.

Jackie grabbed his black gym bag and headed for the door.

'Whoops! I forgot something.' Jackie walked back to Jade's bed and took hold of the top sheet. In one smooth move, he yanked the top sheet out from under Jade – without moving her a single inch.

Jackie saw Jade give a tiny smile. He chuckled to himself. Then he turned and quickly left the room.

An hour later, Jackie sneaked along the roof of the museum. He crouched down beside a large glass skylight and glanced at his watch.

'Eleven o'clock,' he murmured. 'One hour until The Dark Hand arrives.' *Where were Captain Black's agents? Not here*, he thought.

He was on his own. He had to get the snake talisman out before The Dark Hand did.

Jackie peered down at the skylight. A black box with a red light blinked up at him and a red laser beam ran across the window.

It was an alarm. He'd have to turn it off. Jackie grinned. He knew just how to do it.

He reached into his black bag and found some chewing gum. He unwrapped a stick and popped it into his mouth.

'Mmm! Spearmint – my favourite!' he said.

Now for the tricky part.

Jackie wedged the gum's shiny foil wrapper into the skylight. He wiggled the wrapper so that it blocked the laser beam.

The beam hit the shiny foil. Then it bounced back and hit the black alarm box.

The blinking red light switched to a steady green. 'Yes!' Jackie sighed with relief. The alarm was off!

'Oof!' Jackie landed on the

museum floor. The ladder he made with knotted-up bed sheets worked perfectly!

He glanced around. He was in a long hallway. From where he stood, Jackie could see the main exhibit room – where the snake talisman was displayed.

Jackie picked up his bag. He crept quickly down the hall. Just before the door to the exhibit room, he stopped short.

The space was filled with glowing laser beams! The red beams crossed one another in a checkerboard pattern.

Wow! Jackie thought. *This is tough. To get to the talisman, I have to get past the beams. And I can't touch them, or I'll set off an alarm!*

16

Jackie carefully ducked under and over the criss-crossing laser beams.

'Ooh . . . whooo . . . whoa!' Jackie gasped. He wobbled on one foot and swayed to the side.

Only one more beam to go – but he was about to fall!

'Yeeeeow!' He waved his arms in the air. At the last second, he caught his balance – and stepped over the beam without touching it.

Jackie wiped his forehead. Made it! Now for the talisman.

He tiptoed towards the display.

'Hey!' a voice whispered loudly.

'Aaah!' Jackie cried. Someone was in the museum with him!

Chapter 4

A figure stepped out from the shadows.

'Hi, Jackie!' the figure called.

'Jade!' Jackie cried. 'What are you doing here?'

Jade grinned at her uncle. 'I said I wouldn't come *with* you. I didn't say I wouldn't *follow* you. And I did, right around all those beams.'

She glanced around. 'We got in! That is *so* cool!'

Jackie frowned. 'It is *not* cool. It's *breaking the law*! But it's the only way to keep the talisman safe.'

Jackie checked his watch. 'No time to argue now.' He handed his black bag to Jade. Together, they crept up to the talisman.

Jackie took a deep breath. He carefully put one hand on the ancient stone. 'OK. Give me the statue!' he whispered to Jade.

Jade pulled the Statue of Liberty souvenir from the bag and placed it in Jackie's free hand.

There were five lasers pointed at the talisman. If the talisman was removed, the lasers would sense it, and an alarm would go off. But if Jackie switched the talisman with the souvenir fast enough, he might be able to trick the alarm system into thinking the talisman was still there!

Beads of sweat popped out on Jackie's forehead. He held his breath. He steadied his hands. Then, quickly, he lifted the talisman and set the small Statue of Liberty in its place.

No alarm sounded. Yes!

Jade held the black bag open and Jackie dropped the snake talisman into it. 'Time to get out of here!' he said.

Together, Jackie and Jade tiptoed back among the lasers towards the hallway. Jackie noticed his reflection in a mirror on a wall. But wait. Where was Jade's reflection?

Jackie stared hard into the mirror.

'I think that thing is broken,' he said.

Then his mirror image dropped into a fighting stance!

Jackie gasped. This was not his reflection. This was someone else! Someone carrying a black bag, just like his. Dressed all in black, just as he was. Someone ready to attack!

'Ayaah!' the person shouted. It was a woman's voice!

She leaped towards Jackie.

Jackie whirled around, jumped aside and kicked. But his attacker was too fast. The masked figure crouched low, ducking the kick, then sprang at him again.

'Whoa!' Jade exclaimed.

In one smooth move, the attacker

whirled around, kicked out with one leg and hit Jackie in the middle of his back.

'Aahh!' Jackie fell – towards the grid of laser beams!

He braced himself for the wail of the alarms.

'Eerrk!' he croaked. The attacker yanked him back by his collar. She dropped him to the floor – seconds before he broke the beams.

Jackie scrambled to his feet. He pointed to his watch. 'Hey! It's not midnight. You guys are twenty-five minutes early!'

'What guys?' the woman asked. 'There's no one here but us.'

Jackie frowned. 'You mean, you're not with The Dark Hand?'

'No.' The woman pulled off her black ski mask. She shook out her long dark hair. 'My name is Viper.'

Jackie and Jade stared at each other. 'Someone *else* is after the talisman?' they asked each other.

Viper held up her black bag. 'What talisman? I just stole the Pink Puma Diamond.'

'Wow!' Jade cried. 'When I grow up, I want to be just like *her*! She's a female Jackie Chan!'

'She-she is nothing like me!' Jackie sputtered. 'She is a *criminal*!' He stepped in front of Jade.

'*You* are under arrest!' he told Viper.

Viper laughed. 'You realize we'd *both* go to jail, right?'

23

'*I* am not a crook!' Jackie flung up his hands in frustration – and bumped a priceless vase.

The vase flew through the air. Jackie made a desperate grab – too late. The vase hit the floor and smashed into pieces.

At that second, an earsplitting sound filled the museum.

'Oh, no!' Jackie cried out. 'The alarm! Run!'

Jackie grabbed his bag and swooped Jade under his other arm. 'Let's get out of here!' he cried.

Jackie and Viper ran straight through the laser grid. Jackie glanced up. Steel bars slid across the skylight above him. 'Can't go that way,' he said. 'Head for the main doors!'

They turned left and raced towards the front of the museum.

'We have to run faster, Jackie!' Jade

pointed ahead. 'Look!'

Jackie looked – and gasped. More steel bars were slowly closing in front of the main doors. With those blocked, there would be no way to escape!

The steel doors dropped lower . . . and lower.

'Dive!' Jackie shouted. 'Hurry!' Still carrying Jade, he hit the marble floor and skidded across it on his stomach. Viper slid right beside him.

Jackie held his breath.

They slipped under the bars just in time!

The museum's doors sprang open. Jackie, Jade and Viper tumbled on to the front steps.

Viper jumped up. 'Stop following

26

THE SNAKE TALISMAN

The snake talisman has the power of invisibility!

Jade wants to help Jackie find the snake talisman...

...but the search is very dangerous!

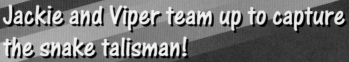

Jackie and Viper team up to capture the snake talisman!

SHENDU
The real leader of The Dark Hand

'There is
no honour
among thieves.'

me, OK?' she told Jackie. She grabbed her bag and raced away.

'No problem,' Jackie replied. He gave Jade his bag and scrambled to his feet. Then he tucked her under his arm again and took off in the other direction.

'Whoa!' Jade exclaimed as Jackie ran down the pavement. She tilted the bag so he could see inside. 'Look! We're rich!'

Jackie glanced down.

At the bottom of the bag sat . . . the Pink Puma Diamond!

'Oh, no!' Jackie yelled. 'Viper took the wrong bag. *She* has the talisman!'

Jackie grabbed the bag. He placed Jade on the pavement. 'Don't go anywhere!' he instructed. 'I have to return the Pink Puma!'

Jackie sped down the pavement and skidded around a corner. He was almost at the museum's steps when five police cars skidded to a halt in front of him.

'Freeze!' a policeman bellowed.

Jackie stopped. He quickly raised his hands in the air.

An officer snatched his bag and opened it. 'Hey – there's nothing in here!' he announced. 'It's empty!'

Huh? Jackie gazed into the bag. It *was* empty. The Pink Puma Diamond had disappeared!

'Chan!' a guard barked out. 'You have a visitor.'

The guard led Jackie from his jail

cell to a small room. Sitting on the other side of a thick plastic barrier was Jade.

'Happy Thanksgiving, Jackie!' she called out happily.

'Jade!' Jackie cried. 'Are you OK?'

Jade nodded and leaned forward. 'The Big Meow is comfy-cosy,' she whispered.

Jackie frowned. 'What is that supposed to mean?'

'The cat is in the bag.' Jade winked.

'*What?*' Jackie asked.

Jade rolled her eyes. 'I have the Pink Puma!' she said. 'I slipped it into my pocket when you weren't looking. I guess I sort of "pulled a Viper".'

Jackie frowned. 'Well, don't pull any more Vipers!' he whispered back. 'She's a bad influence! In fact, I want you to hand the Puma over to the police, right now!'

'I didn't bring it *here*,' Jade said. 'We need it to get the talisman back. I'm going to find Viper and arrange a trade!'

'Jade!' Jackie cried. 'Captain Black should be here soon to bail me out. When he does, *I* will find Viper.'

'You get to do all the fun stuff,' Jade complained.

'This is serious, Jade,' Jackie told her. 'I still don't know what magical power the snake talisman has. Viper – or the entire city – could be in great danger because of it!'

Chapter 6

Viper sat on a couch in her flat. She smiled as she read the front page of the newspaper. The very first story was about Jackie Chan's arrest.

Viper laughed. 'Chan returned to the scene of the crime! Why would he do a stupid thing like that?'

She grabbed her black bag from the coffee table. She opened it – and froze.

The Pink Puma Diamond wasn't inside!

Instead, her bag held Chan's snake talisman!

I must have taken Chan's bag by mistake, she realized.

She grabbed the talisman and squeezed it hard. 'What am I supposed to do with *this*?' she grumbled.

Zap! A bright light came from under her fingers. She opened her fist and looked at the talisman. It was glowing!

'What *is* this thing?' Viper wondered. She raised her eyes – and gasped. A huge mirror hung on the wall across from her. She should have seen her reflection in it. But her reflection wasn't there!

The talisman's power made her invisible!

'Wow!' Viper murmured. She squeezed the talisman again. Her reflection appeared.

Viper squeezed the talisman and became invisible again. *Now you see me. Now you don't!* she thought.

Back at the jail, Ratso waited for Jackie Chan to enter the visitors' room. He glanced down and smiled.

In his lap he held a special compass called The Seeker. The wand had four fierce-looking dragon heads at the top. When The Seeker sensed that a talisman was near, one of the dragon heads glowed red, pointing out the right direction.

All Ratso had to do was aim The Seeker at Chan. If Chan had the talisman, Ratso could take it from him! That would put him in Valmont's good books – at least for a little while.

The door opened. Chan frowned when he saw Ratso. 'What are *you* doing here?' he asked as he sat down.

Ratso leaned close to the plastic barrier. 'Where's the snake talisman?' he demanded loudly.

'Oh!' Chan smiled innocently. 'Don't you read the newspapers? I didn't take the snake. I took the Pink Puma.'

Huh? Ratso quickly held up The Seeker. It wasn't glowing.

'See?' Chan said. 'No talisman, like

34

the gizmo says. Now I have to go.' He got up and strolled to the door.

Ratso gritted his teeth. 'I'll find it!' he called angrily as Chan left the room. 'It's just a matter of time!'

Ratso left the police station and hurried down the pavement. *If Chan doesn't have the talisman, where is it?* he wondered.

Then he stopped short. The Seeker was glowing – pointing south! It had found the talisman!

Ratso glanced around excitedly. But no one else was on the pavement with him. He checked The Seeker again. Now a different dragon head was glowing – pointing to the west.

But no one was there!

Jackie paced nervously in his cell. He had to get out of there and find the talisman before Ratso did!

Jackie heard a jingling sound outside his cell. He turned around.

What? A ring full of keys was floating down the hall – by itself!

Clink. One of the keys went into the lock of his cell. The cell door swung open. 'Hey there, Chan,' a woman's voice murmured.

Jackie gulped. 'Viper?'

'The one and only,' Viper said. 'And I discovered your talisman's secret power.'

'Really? What does it – oh!' Jackie shrugged. Of course! This talisman could make people invisible!

36

'Come on,' Viper told him. 'Let's bust you out of here.'

'No!' Jackie protested. 'I don't want to be busted out!'

'You want your snake toy back, don't you?' Viper warned. 'Or should I just sell it?'

No! Jackie thought. *If I let that happen, The Dark Hand will get the talisman for sure!* He had no choice. He left the cell and started down the hall.

As soon as Jackie and Viper got far enough away from the jail, Viper made herself visible. Then she led Jackie through the city streets. They walked under the shadow of a rusty old bridge.

'Pssst!' someone whispered.

Jackie jumped. He and Viper turned.

A small figure in a big hat and trenchcoat stood before them.

'Jade!' Jackie gasped. '*You* set this up?'

Jade nodded. Then she looked at Viper. 'Did you bring the goods?' she asked in a phoney gruff voice.

'This is not a good idea,' Jackie declared. 'Trading in stolen goods is against the law!'

Viper raised an eyebrow. 'You want the talisman?'

Jackie groaned. 'OK,' he agreed. 'Just hurry – before The Dark Hand finds us.'

Jade took the Pink Puma from her

coat pocket. Viper pulled out the snake talisman. Quickly, they made the trade.

Viper slipped the diamond into her pocket. 'You're all right, Jade.' She winked at Jade and then walked away.

Jade dropped the talisman into Jackie's hand. 'You should ask Viper out on a date!' she said. 'She'd be such a cool aunt!'

'Jade...' Jackie started to say. But then he realized something. The talisman was too light! He squeezed it. It crumbled into pieces!

'Jade, look! This isn't the real talisman!' Jackie cried. 'It's a fake! Viper tricked us!'

Jade stared at the pieces of the

phoney talisman. 'Viper…pulled a Viper?' she asked. 'On *me?*'

Jackie squeezed her shoulder. 'Old proverb: "There is no honour among thieves." Let's find her, Jade.'

Jade nodded grimly. 'Yeah. Let's get her!'

Chapter 7

The Thanksgiving Day Parade was in full swing outside Viper's building. Balloons floated, bands marched, music blared – but Viper hardly noticed. Now she had the Pink Puma Diamond *and* the snake talisman!

Viper stepped inside her flat – and gasped.

A man with blond hair and cold blue eyes sat on her couch.

41

'Who are you?' Viper demanded.

'My name is Valmont,' the man replied. He stood up and held out a hand. 'The talisman, please.'

Viper shook her head. 'It's not for sale.'

Valmont sneered. 'I didn't intend to buy it.' He snapped his fingers. A group of black-clad ninjas swarmed into the room.

Viper quickly pulled out the talisman and squeezed it. Now she was invisible. 'Can't have what you can't see!' she teased.

She gripped the talisman, opened her balcony door and jumped on to the ledge of her building.

'After her!' she heard Valmont cry.

Jackie and Jade stood on the crowded street. 'Hey, Jackie! Check it out!' Jade cried. She pointed up at the ledge of a nearby building.

Jackie looked up. A bunch of shadowy figures was swarming on to the ledge. *Shadowkhan*, he thought with a shiver. The Dark Hand's fierce, mysterious warriors.

The Shadowkhan were kicking, punching, whirling and ducking. They seemed to be fighting with nothing. But Jackie knew better.

Viper is up there too, he thought. *She has the talisman. And the Shadowkhan are after it! I have to get to it first!*

Jackie gestured towards the street. 'Look, Jade, you get to watch the parade after all!' he said excitedly.

'Now you wait right here, OK? I'll get you a soda!'

Jackie left Jade on the pavement and ran down the street. Ahead of him he saw a group of people holding thick cables. The cables were attached to a gigantic moose-shaped parade balloon. The balloon floated high above the crowd.

Jackie had an idea. He grabbed the cables from the balloon walkers' hands and kept on running. 'Sorry-I'll-bring-it-right-back-thank-you!' he shouted.

Jackie's feet left the ground. He swung into the air.

The moose balloon began to float up the side of Viper's building. Hand over hand, Jackie hoisted himself up a cable. Finally, he climbed on to the moose's head.

'Oh, no!' Viper shouted from above.

Jackie looked up. A small object tumbled from the ledge and landed with a plop on top of the balloon's nose.

The talisman! Jackie crawled towards it.

'Heads up!' Viper screamed.

Now she was tumbling through the air!

Thump! She hit the surface of the balloon.

'Whoa!' Jackie bounced high into the air.

When he landed, Viper was beside him. Viper had the talisman in her

45

hand. She tossed it to Jackie. 'Here. It's yours.'

'Make sure it's real this time!' a voice called out.

Jackie whirled around. Jade was perched on the moose's shoulders! *How did she get up there?* Jackie wondered.

Jade gasped. 'Uh-oh! Company!'

Jackie turned. Three Shadowkhan were crawling over the moose's head. Two more jumped on near the nose, bouncing Jackie into the air. The talisman flew from his grasp. He caught it between his teeth and landed in a fighting stance.

The battle was on!

With lightning speed, Jackie and Viper fought the Shadowkhan.

They bounced, booted and punched them off the balloon.

But the Shadowkhan kept coming.

Jackie grasped the talisman. *Wham!* One of the Shadowkhan kicked Jackie's hand. The talisman began to glow.

Wow! I'm invisible! Jackie realized.

'Hey, over here!' he teased the Shadowkhan, bouncing around the balloon. 'I'm here!' He bounced away. 'No, I'm here! Or could I be here?'

Wham! A Shadowkhan landed a lucky kick on Jackie's fingers. The talisman flew into the air – and the Shadowkhan caught it!

Now the ninja was invisible, and Jackie wasn't!

Uh-oh, Jackie thought. *I'm in trouble!*

'Hey, Jackie!' Jade shouted. She grabbed a paint bucket from a balcony on the building beside her. She swung the bucket and ... *splash!* The ninja reappeared – covered in dripping green paint.

The green Shadowkhan jumped to his feet.

'Ayaah!' Viper leaped up and bounced him from the balloon.

As he soared through the air, the talisman dropped from his hand.

'I've got it!' Jackie cried. He caught the talisman and shoved it into his pocket.

The green ninja now stood on the ledge of a nearby building.

He held something glittering in his hands.

Jackie squinted. Uh-oh. Ninja stars! Those weapons were sharp! They could put a big hole in the moose balloon!

Zing! The ninja threw one of the stars. Jackie grabbed the empty paint bucket. *Clank!* The star landed inside.

Three more stars zipped furiously through the air. Jackie caught them all. But a final star sailed over the bucket.

Pop! The star sank deep into the moose balloon. *Sssss!* Air hissed loudly. The moose balloon began to zoom through the streets!

'Aaahhh!' Jackie, Jade and Viper yelled. They hung on tightly as the moose zipped between buildings. It touched the treetops. It soared over a bridge.

'I can't watch!' Jackie yelled. He squeezed his eyes shut.

Whomp! The balloon landed.

Now where are we? Jackie wondered. He opened his eyes. Far below, he saw water and boats and ... a big green foot?

Whoa! The balloon had landed on top of the Statue of Liberty!

'At least I'm seeing the sights in New York,' Jade said.

Just then, the talisman slipped from Jackie's pocket! It tumbled down through the air – and landed between two of the statue's toes.

It was a very tight fit. So tight that

the talisman began to glow. And the Statue of Liberty became invisible!

'Sights? I don't see any sights,' Viper joked.

Chapter 8

A few minutes later, Jackie, Jade and Viper were on the ground below the Statue of Liberty. Curious crowds pointed at the empty space where the famous statue should be.

Police sirens sounded in the far distance. 'I guess that's my cue to exit,' Viper announced. She pocketed the Pink Puma. Then she turned to Jackie and Jade. 'Thanks for the save back there. I owe you one.' She winked and strolled quickly away.

'Then give me back the Puma!' Jackie called after her. 'I have to return it. The police think I took it. Please!'

Viper disappeared into the crowd.

Jackie sighed.

'Uh, Jackie?' Jade said. 'I know you told me never to "pull a Viper" again, but, well...she owed you one.'

Jade held out her hand. She had the Pink Puma Diamond!

Jackie picked it up. 'What...how?' he sputtered.

A dozen police officers surrounded Jackie and his niece. 'Freeze!' an officer shouted.

'It's OK!' Jackie cried. He put the

Pink Puma on the ground and stepped back. 'I didn't steal it! I don't want it! It's yours!'

The officer picked up the diamond. 'Fine,' he declared. 'Now – tell us what you did with the Statue of Liberty!'

Jackie looked back at where the statue should be. The snake talisman was still stuck between the statue's toes, he realized.

'Oops!' He chuckled. 'Sorry.' He walked towards the statue. 'Looks like it's time for one more reappearing act!'

A letter to you from Jackie

Dear Friends

In *Enter . . . the Viper*, Jade thinks it's really cool that I took the talisman from the museum. Sometimes for my job I have to return stolen objects to their rightful owners. It's never cool to take something that doesn't belong to you. Being cool never involves breaking the law.

Jade also says she wants to be just like Viper when she grows up. Viper is strong and clever and she's really good at martial arts. Jade even calls her a female Jackie.

Then I explain to Jade that Viper made a bad choice. And I tell Jade an old saying I learned as a kid: there is no honour among thieves.

A friend once said that if I was not a successful movie star, I would be a very good burglar because I have lots of energy and I can jump over walls with ease.

I still laugh when I think about that. My skills would never get in the way of my beliefs as a person. Being an honourable person is very important to me. Thieves have no honour, so I could never be one.

But having honour is not always easy. It takes

courage to believe that good things will happen to good people. And this courage is what got me where I am today.

When I was a teenager, the boarding school I went to closed down. I had lived there for most of my life. My parents were in another country. I was left to take care of myself with no one to help me.

I was scared and alone. It would have been very easy for me to get involved with a bad crowd and go down the wrong path.

But I didn't. I set a goal for myself. I wanted to become an actor. So I used the skills I learned at school, worked as hard as I could and climbed my way to the top. It took years and years, but I finally made it.

Now that I'm successful, I do the exact opposite of stealing. I give. Giving to charity is a big part of my life.

In the end, Jade realized one of life's little secrets: just because you *have* the ability to do something doesn't mean you *should*. You may be tempted to take the easy way out, but the harder road is often the better one.